The King of Tiny Things

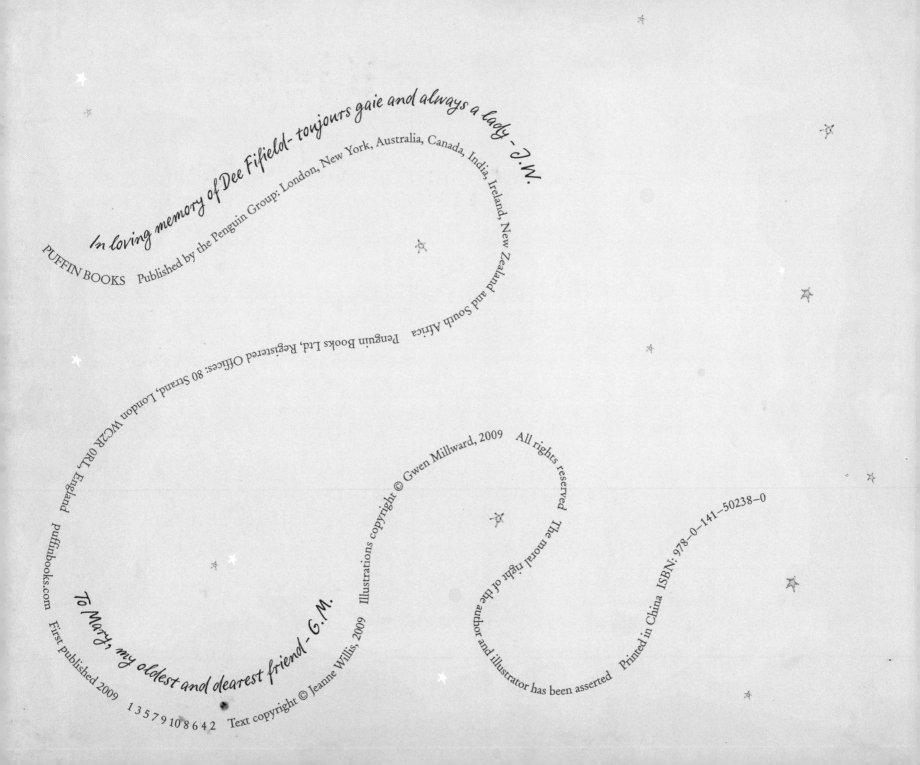

In loving memory of Dee Fifield- toujours gaie and always a lady - J.W.

PUFFIN BOOKS   Published by the Penguin Group: London, New York, Australia, Canada, India, Ireland, New Zealand and South Africa   Penguin Books Ltd, Registered Offices: 80 Strand, London WC2R 0RL England

puffinbooks.com   First published 2009   1 3 5 7 9 10 8 6 4 2   Text copyright © Jeanne Willis, 2009   Illustrations copyright © Gwen Millward, 2009   All rights reserved   The moral right of the author and illustrator has been asserted   Printed in China ISBN: 978-0-141-50238-0

To Mary, my oldest and dearest friend - G.M.

The King of Tiny Things

Written by Jeanne Willis   Illustrated by Gwen Millward

PUFFIN

*O*ne summer, when we were small,
we went to stay with Nana and Grandad.

There was a tent in Grandad's shed.
"You could camp under the stars," he said.

*I*t seemed like a brilliant idea until bedtime.
We'd only ever slept indoors with the light on.
"Night, night. Sleep tight," they said.

We didn't. Daren't - too dark!

I shone my torch. "Don't!" said Chrissy.

"Creepy Crawlies will come and get us."

There was a fuzzy shadow. Something mothy crept in through the flap.

Chrissy screamed. She swatted it on to its back. But it wasn't a bug . . .

*I*t was a boy no bigger than a beetle.
He looked us in the eye and he sang this lullaby,

"I am the King of Tiny Things,
Who creep and crawl or buzz their wings.
Mine is the magic that night-time brings,
Follow me, follow me, follow me!"

He led us up the garden path and disappeared under the shed.
We looked and there he was, oiling a slug who'd lost its slime.

"Eeugh!" said Chrissy.
"How can you care for
Creepy Crawlies?"

"How can you not?" he cried.
"They turn the soil so seeds can sow. They visit plants so crops can grow.

We need them more than you could know . . . *Follow me, follow me, follow me!*"

So when the
King of Tiny Things
found a worm drying on the path,
we carried it to the
compost heap to recover.

When he found a caterpillar trapped
under a pot, we set it free.

And when he found a daddy-long-legs missing a leg,
we made it a new one.

The king showed us many
marvellous moonlit things.

Weevils with copper wings.

Chubby grubs. Badger cubs.

Baby bats in furry hats.

But best of all, he showed
  us that even in the shadows
the night was bright with magic, and he sang,

"... *Follow me, follow me, follow me!*"

We didn't follow him straight away,
we were too busy being brave but we should have.

His boat had sunk. We fished him out of the pond.

If his heart was beating, I couldn't feel it.
It was smaller than an apple pip.

I tried to give him the kiss of life but Chrissy said,
"Stop! He is no bigger than a beetle.
We must nurse him the Creepy Crawly way."

She found a reed no wider than a whisker and put it to his lips.
   "I'll give him little puffs," she said. "You pinch his nose."

I pinched and she puffed. She pinched and I puffed,
   and he spluttered, sat up and looked
very pleased to be alive.

As we tucked him into bed, he shivered and he said,

"For the love of Tiny Things, will you be my Creepy Crawly Queens?"

"Yes!" we said.
"But you must rest now, little man.
Night night. Sleep tight."

We woke early.
We went to say goodbye to him
before Dad came to fetch us.
Chrissy got there first.
She was kneeling by his bed with
her head in her hands.
All that was left of him was his crown,
his cloak and his crumpled skin.
"Fetch a matchbox," she cried,
"and a trowel."

We buried the matchbox under a marigold. But as we turned to leave, something flew down and landed on my hand.

At first I thought it was a beetle, but it wasn't . . .

It was the King of Tiny Things . . .

only bigger, bolder, brighter.

As if he'd shed his skin to get his grown-up wings.

And by the moon and the stars,
he smiled and he sang . . .

"Follow me,

follow me,

follow me!"

★ And on those magical summer nights ★
when we stayed with Nana and Grandad,
★ that's just what we did. ★ ★

$\mathcal{T}$his is to certify that on the ...... day of the ...... month in the year ....

(NAME) .... (AGE)...................

was awarded the title of:

$\mathcal{C}$HIEF ASSISTANT TO THE $\mathcal{K}$ING OF TINY THINGS

FOR IDENTIFYING THE CREATURES BELOW

AND PROMISING TO PROTECT THEM

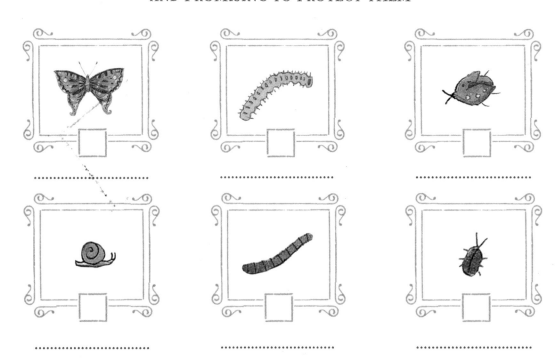

....

....

ALSO FOR STUDYING A CREEPY CRAWLY OF THEIR CHOICE AND SENDING A DRAWING TO THE KING.

Please send your drawings and research to the King of Tiny Things at the following address:
Puffin Picture Books, 80 Strand, London WC2R 0RL